Something Is Wrong at My House

REVISED EDITION

A Book About Parents' Fighting

Diane Davis | illustrated by Keith R. Neely

Parenting Press
Chicago

Acknowledgments

I would like to thank Elizabeth Crary for publishing the original version of *Something Is Wrong at My House,* for continuing to believe in its message, and for agreeing to its revision. Thanks too to Carolyn Threadgill for her encouragement, support, and editorial expertise throughout the revision process. Special thanks to the late Joan Misenar, whose understanding and wise counsel led me back to my writing and inspired the work I have been doing ever since.

• • •

First published in 1984, copyright © by Diane Davis

Revised in 2010, text copyright © by Diane Davis; illustrations © by Parenting Press

Printed in the United States of America

Library of Congress Cartaloging-in-Publication Data

Davis, Diane, 1948-
  Something is wrong at my house : a book about parents' fighting
Diane Davis ; illustrated by Keith R. Neely. -- Rev. ed.
     p. cm.
  Summary: A boy who lives with domestic violence finally has the courage
to speak to an adult and ask for help.
  ISBN 978-1-884734-65-6 (pbk.) -- ISBN 978-1-884734-66-3 (library binding)
[1. Family violence--Fiction. 2. Parents--Fiction. 3. Schools--Fiction.] I. Neely, Keith, 1943- ill. II. Title.
  PZ7.D28587So 2010
  [E]--dc22
                        2009050159

Parenting Press
814 North Franklin Street
Chicago, Illinois 60610
ISBN 978-1-884734-65-6

Introduction

The purpose of *Something Is Wrong at My House* is to help break the generational cycle of domestic violence. Since domestic violence stems from *learned* behavior and affects 3.3 million children per year, the best place to start is with the youngest generation, the children. We must let them know that domestic violence is *not* the norm in families, allow them to talk about their feelings, and teach them skills that will help them deal with conflict in nonviolent ways.

The book is based on a true story about a boy living in a violent household. He experiences the universal feelings of fear, anger, and hopelessness common to victims of domestic violence. In the story he is able to identify his feelings and find appropriate ways to cope with them. He also seeks outside help by confiding in his teacher.

Something Is Wrong at My House helps all children, those from violent and nonviolent homes, by giving them permission to have their feelings and suggesting appropriate ways they can act on them. Some children will choose to channel their feelings in physical ways, whereas others will prefer to be quiet and spend time alone so they can "re-set."

Teachers can read this nonthreatening story to their students and present ways that children can cope and stay safe if they are living in violent homes. Counselors can use the book to help children identify their feelings, teach coping skills, and discuss a Safety Plan. Parents can learn how deeply children are affected by domestic violence, and use the story to talk to their children about it.

The format of the book is designed to permit use with both preschool and school-aged children. The longer text on the left was written for the older children; the shorter captions beneath the illustrations are directed toward younger children.

Domestic violence is painful. As children learn to identify their feelings and learn new, positive ways of expressing them, they can begin to break the cycle of violence.

Something's wrong at my house.

My mom and dad have terrible fights. Sometimes they yell and shout. Sometimes they don't talk to each other for days. Other times my dad threatens my mom and she cries. Often they push, hit, kick, and even throw things.

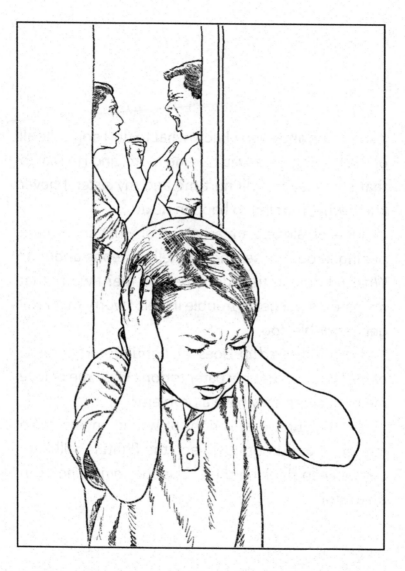

My mommy and daddy have terrible fights.

It *scares* me and I don't know what to do. I don't like all of the hurting. I see Dad hurting Mom, and I'm scared that someday he will hurt me and my sister. I never know what is going to happen next.

I feel all alone. I am ashamed of what keeps happening at our house. Should I tell someone about it? What if I do and they don't believe me? I worry that my parents will get in trouble if I tell. I worry that I will get in trouble, too.

I also *feel mixed up*. Does the fighting start because of me? Is it because my parents don't want me or love me or because they have a problem?

I'm not sure what is right or wrong anymore. No matter what I do or how I act, the fighting still happens. I keep thinking there must be *something* I can do to stop it.

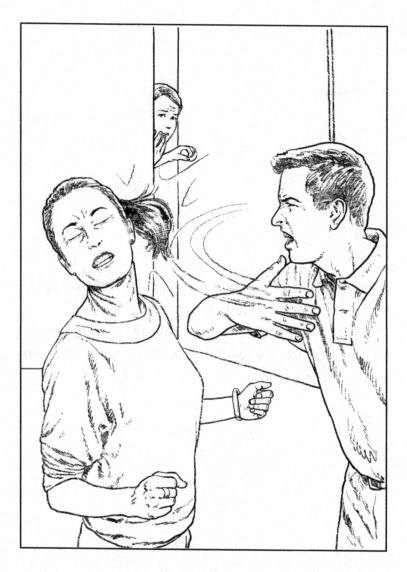

It scares me and I don't know what to do.
Do they fight because they have a problem?

I get so worried that sometimes I can't sleep at night. When I do sleep I have bad dreams.

Being worried makes me want to run away or hide or *grow up fast* so I can protect myself and my mom and my little sister.

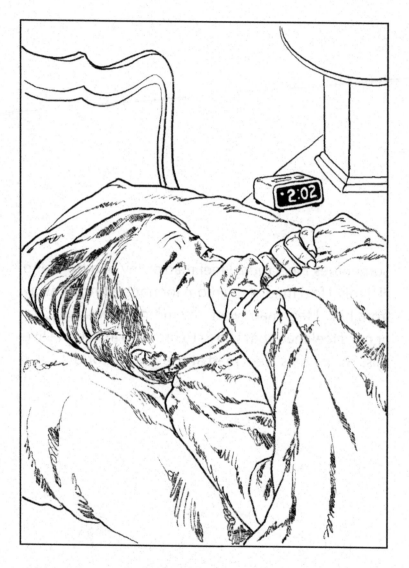

I get so worried that sometimes I have
bad dreams.

Sometimes I feel *mad*. I feel mad at my dad for being like this. I feel mad at my mom for not getting us away from him. I feel mad when my mom yells at my sister or me. I feel mad that I have to grow up in a home like this. Sometimes I feel mad at the whole world!

I am mad that I have to grow up in a
home like this.

I get so mad that I feel like I might explode. I want to hit my dad back for hurting my mom. I feel like hitting my mom whenever she says "No" to me. I pick on my little sister until she cries. I kick my dog and tease my cat. Sometimes I lie about where I'm going and what I've been doing.

When I'm mad I pick on my little sister.

Lately I've been having trouble at school. When I'm worried about what's happening at home I can't pay attention in class. Instead of doing my own work, I copy other people's answers. I talk back to my teacher and start fights with my friends. Sometimes I even take other people's things.

At recess I don't feel like having fun with the other kids. If I'm mad, I bully some of them. If I'm feeling worried or sad, I cry a lot. Lots of times I just go off by myself so I won't have to be around anyone.

At school I have trouble, too.

One day I asked Mom why she and Dad fight so much. She said, "We are going through a tough time right now, but we will work things out." But they *aren't* working things out. Things just keep getting worse.

I wish we could be a happy family. I want the fighting to stop. I don't like all the hurting. I don't want to feel mad, scared, ashamed, and mixed up anymore.

I wish we could be a happy family.

What can I do?

My teacher says that kids need to think of good ways to get rid of their mad feelings without hitting or being mean to anyone. I made a list of things I can do outside. It says:

- Take deep breaths
- Play with my dog
- Shoot baskets
- Ride my skateboard
- Throw a ball against a wall
- Jump rope
- Climb a tree
- Ride my bike or scooter
- Swing on my swing set

I can get rid of some of the mad feelings in me without hitting.

To make myself feel happy when I'm inside I can:

- Take deep breaths
- Talk to a friend
- Cuddle with my cat
- Listen to music
- Work on a puzzle
- Draw or paint
- Read a book
- Play my favorite video game

And I can do something that makes
me happy.

I can also talk to a grown-up whom I like and trust.

I could choose my teacher, the school nurse or counselor, my babysitter, soccer coach, pastor, or my best friend's mom, but I'm not sure what to say.

What can I say to them?

I can also talk to a grown-up.

Maybe I will try talking to my neighbor.

Chris: Something is wrong at my house.
Mrs. Brown: What is it, Chris?
Chris: My dad keeps hitting my mom.
Mrs. Brown: Oh, it can't be that bad. It isn't any of my
    business anyway.

I guess she doesn't believe me. What shall I do now?

I can talk to my neighbor.

Who else might listen? I will try my teacher.

Chris: Something is wrong at my house. My dad keeps hitting my mom and hurting her. What can I do to make him stop?

Ms. Cortez: Oh, Chris, I am so sorry this is happening at your house. Your dad is the only one who can get himself to stop hitting, not you. It's important for you to take care of *yourself* and stay safe. Have you talked to your mom about what's happening and how you feel?

Chris: Yes, but she says she and Dad are going through a tough time right now and that things will get better. They *aren't* getting better though. They're just getting worse!

Ms. Cortez: I am glad you have come to ask me for help. I will talk to someone else who will be able to help you and your sister and your mom. Let's talk again tomorrow so I can tell you what I've found out.

I can talk to my teacher.

The next day, my teacher talked to me and explained that what's going on at my house is called *domestic violence*. She said that it happens in all kinds of families, but some kids are too scared or too ashamed to tell anyone else about it.

"You did the right thing by telling me," she said. "That took a lot of courage, and I am proud of you."

She also said, "Please remember that the hitting is *not* your fault. Your parents need help, and there are places where they can get it. The lady I talked to yesterday will call your mother and tell her about these places."

A grown-up will call my mommy
to help her.

Today my teacher talked to our class about having a Safety Plan. She asked us these questions:

- Where can you go inside your house to feel safe?
- Where can you go outside your house to feel safe?
- Who is an adult in your family that you can go to for help?
- Who is an adult outside your family that you can go to for help?
- Do you know how to dial 911 and what to say to the person who answers? Practice saying this:
  *My name is*_____.
  *My phone number is*_____.
  (include area code)
  *My address is*_____.
  (street and city address)
  I need help because Mommy and Daddy are fighting.

Stay on the phone until the grown-up at 911 tells you to hang up.

I didn't know about having a Safety Plan before. I thought about the questions and answered them. Now I have my very own Safety Plan!

I have my own Safety Plan!

Since talking to my teacher I have been trying new ways to take care of me. Some of them are:

- Getting out my mad feelings in safe ways
- Doing things that make me happy
- Talking to grown-ups I trust

I am a very special, lovable person.
My needs are important.
I deserve to be safe and happy, and so do you!